his book belongs to:

D0994674

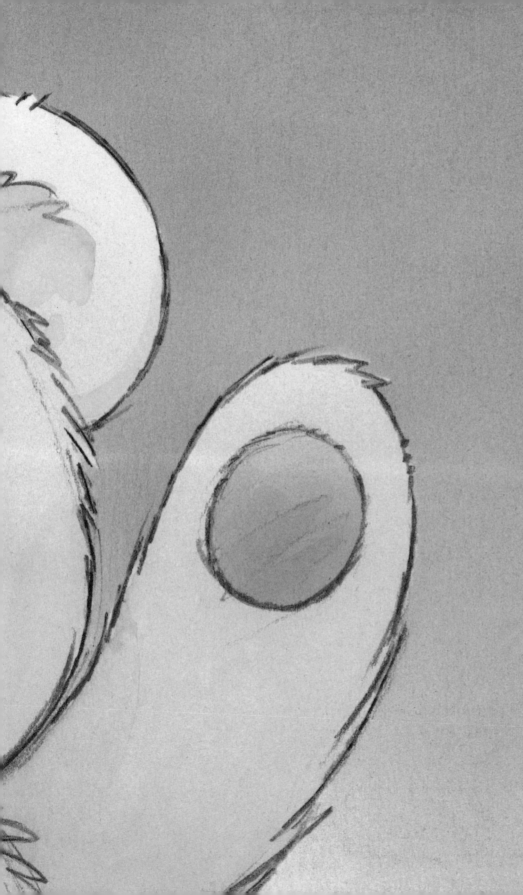

For Vicki, Lily, Edward and Tilly

Rockpool Children's Books
15 North Street
Marton
Warwickshire
CV23 9RJ

First published in Great Britain by Rockpool Children's Books Ltd. 2006
Text and Illustrations copyright © Stuart Trotter 2006
Stuart Trotter has asserted the moral rights
to be identified as the author and illustrator of this book.

ISBN 0-9553022-2-6
ISBN 978-0-9553022-2-0

Printed in China

Stuart Trotter

My Perfect Pet

rockpool©
children's books

My perfect pet...

is dry, not wet,

is not

too small...

...and not too **tall**

He's not too hairy...

and not too scary!

He's not
too grimey...

and not too slimey!

Not too leathery,

...and not too feathery.

He's not too jumpy...

and not too bumpy.

He's
not
too
slinky...

and not too stinky!

He's not too cheeky...

and not
too squeaky.

He's not too spiny...

and not at all shiny!

He's not too snappy...

but is very happy!

Can you guess what I've got?

I'm sure you'll never have met...

such a wonderfully...

perfect pet!